For Gemk,

Whose endless supply of ideas and honest critique made this possible.

感謝 Gemk

源源不絕的靈感及誠懇的建議讓這一切成真。

The Jelly Doughnut That Lost Its Jelly

失去果醬的果醬甜甜圈

Coleen Reddy 著

倪 靖 繪

薛慧儀 譯

三民書局

In a bakery, the jelly doughnuts were waiting to be bought.
One jelly doughnut, Jim, was looking at himself in the shop window.
He was a handsome doughnut.

在一家麵包店裡，有很多果醬甜甜圈等著被買走。
其中有一個叫做吉姆的果醬甜甜圈，正看著自己在店裡玻璃窗上的倒影。
他是一個長得很帥的甜甜圈。

Jim was perfectly round. He was golden in color.

He had just the right amount of sugar sprinkled on him.

But the best part, of course, was his little center of delicious strawberry jelly.

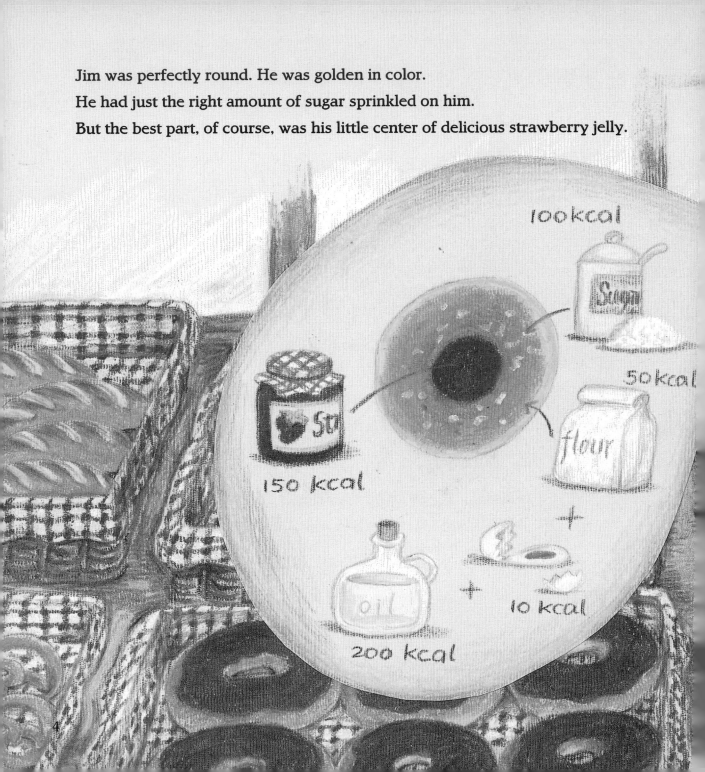

100kcal

50 kcal

150 kcal

200 kcal

10 kcal

吉姆的身材是弧度非常完美的正圓形。

在他金黃色的身上，糖粉不多不少撒得剛剛好。

當然，最棒的部份，還是他肚子上那美味的草莓果醬囉！

5

He was sure that he was the BEST jelly doughnut.
Someone would come into the bakery and buy him.
He was surely the yummiest jelly doughnut.

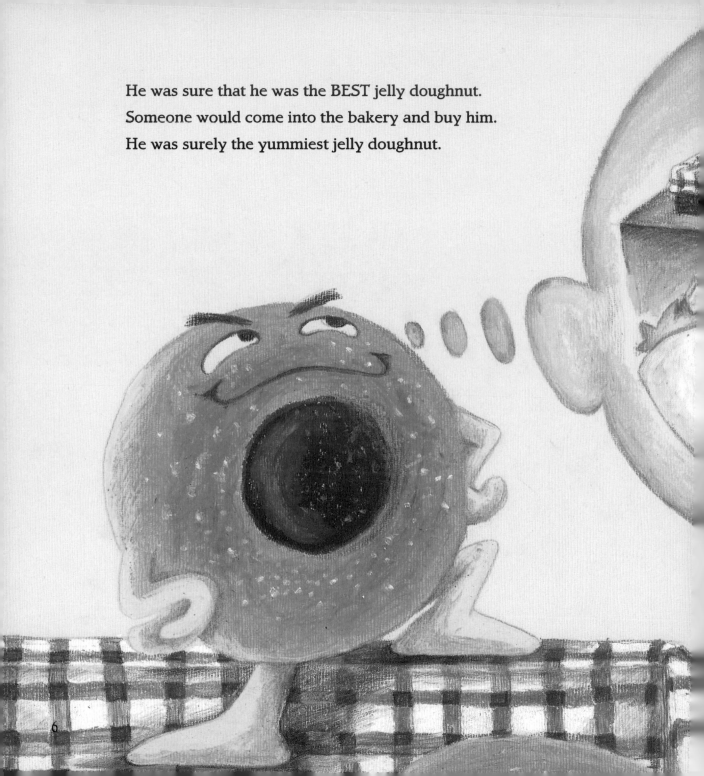

他深信自己是最正點的果醬甜甜圈，
一定會有人走進麵包店裡把他買走。
他絕對是最美味可口的果醬甜甜圈。

But no one came into the bakery that day.

"Maybe tomorrow," thought Jim.

He fell asleep.

但是那天卻沒人走進麵包店裡。
「也許明天就會有人把我買走了吧！」吉姆這樣想。
然後他就睡著了。

When Jim woke up the next morning, he felt a little strange.
He felt like something was missing.
He looked at himself in the shop window.

第二天早晨，吉姆醒過來時，覺得有點兒怪怪的，
好像，有什麼東西不見了。
他在麵包店的玻璃窗前看著自己。

Yes, there was his sugar and... what?

Where was his jelly?

It wasn't real.

12

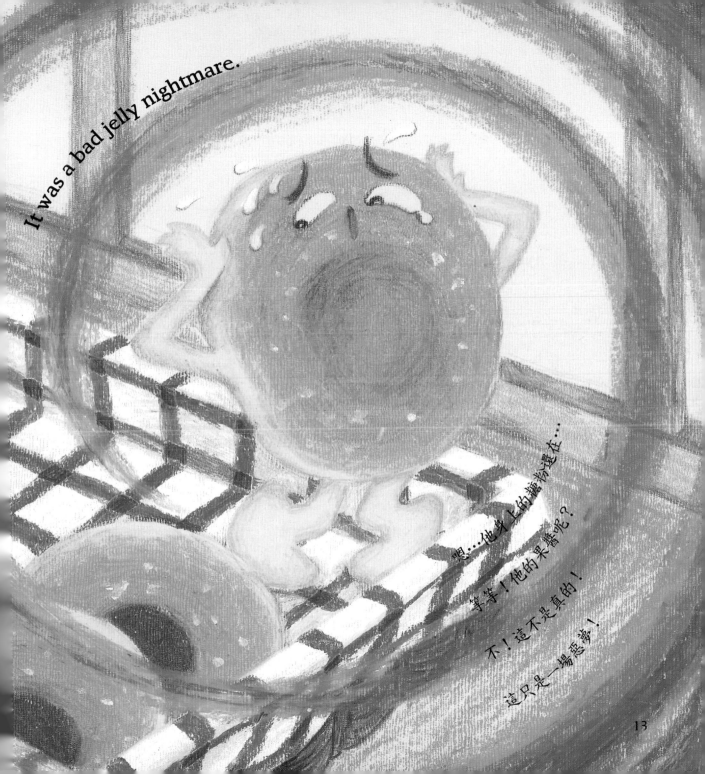

It was a bad jelly nightmare.

嗯…他身上的糖粉還在…

等等！他的果醬呢？

不！這不是真的！

這只是一場惡夢！

13

His jelly was gone. It was missing! He started to cry.
Who would buy a jelly doughnut without any jelly?
The other jelly doughnuts started laughing at him.
"A jelly doughnut without jelly! What a joke!"
they said, pointing to him.

他的果醬不見了！不知道去哪兒了！吉姆哭了起來。
誰會買一個沒有果醬的果醬甜甜圈呢？其他的果醬
甜甜圈開始嘲笑他。「一個沒有果醬的果醬甜甜圈！
笑死人囉！」他們指著他說。

"It is not a joke," said the Apple Pie. "I know who did it."

"You mean some nasty person stole my jelly?" asked Jim.

"Yes, the baker's son always comes in here and eats the jelly but not the doughnut," said the Apple Pie.

「這一點也不好笑,我知道是誰做的。」蘋果派說。
「你是說,有個可惡的人偷走了我的果醬?」吉姆問。
「沒錯!麵包師傅的兒子總是跑進來這裡,把果醬吃掉,
留下空空的甜甜圈。」蘋果派說。

"Oh how cruel! How could he leave me half eaten?"
cried Jim. "Boo Hoo Hoo...."
"Now no one will want me. I'll die and then I'll get thrown
away in the tr...tr...trashcan."
Now it was the strangest thing. All the food in the bakery
was not afraid of being eaten but was afraid of the trashcan.

18

「天哪！真是太殘忍了！他怎麼可以只吃一半就把我丟下呢？
嗚嗚嗚…」吉姆哭著說。「現在沒有人會要我了。我會死掉，
然後被扔進垃、垃、垃圾桶裡了啦！」
這真是一件奇怪的事。所有麵包店裡的食物都不怕被吃掉，
只怕被扔進垃圾桶裡。

19

"We'll fix you," said the Apple Pie.

"You cannot fix me. It's over. I'm going to die without my jelly.

Hold my hand as I die," said Jim.

"People go to a doctor when they're sick.

We'll take you to a doctor," said the Apple Pie.

「我們會把你治好的。」蘋果派說。
「你治不好我的，我完了！沒有果醬，我就活不下去了。
我死掉的時候，拜託你握著我的手。」吉姆說。
「人生病的時候都會去看醫生，我們也可以帶你去看醫生。」蘋果派說。

"Where can we find a doctor?" asked Jim.

"There's a doctor next door. I have heard the baker talking about him," said the Apple Pie.

"You know so much. You must have been here a long time," said Jim. "Why didn't anyone buy you?"

"Because I'm not real, you idiot. I'm plastic," said the Apple Pie.

「到哪裡可以找到醫生呀?」吉姆問。

「我聽麵包師傅說過,隔壁就有個醫生唷。」蘋果派說。

「你知道得真多耶!你一定在這裡待了很久吧?

為什麼沒有人要買你呢?」吉姆說。

「笨蛋,因為我不是真的,我是塑膠做的啦!」蘋果派回答。

The Apple Pie and Jim went next door to the doctor.

They lay down on the doctor's bed.

The doctor came in and got a shock.

於是蘋果派和吉姆來到隔壁的診所找醫生。
他們躺在醫生的床上等著。
醫生進來時，嚇了一大跳。

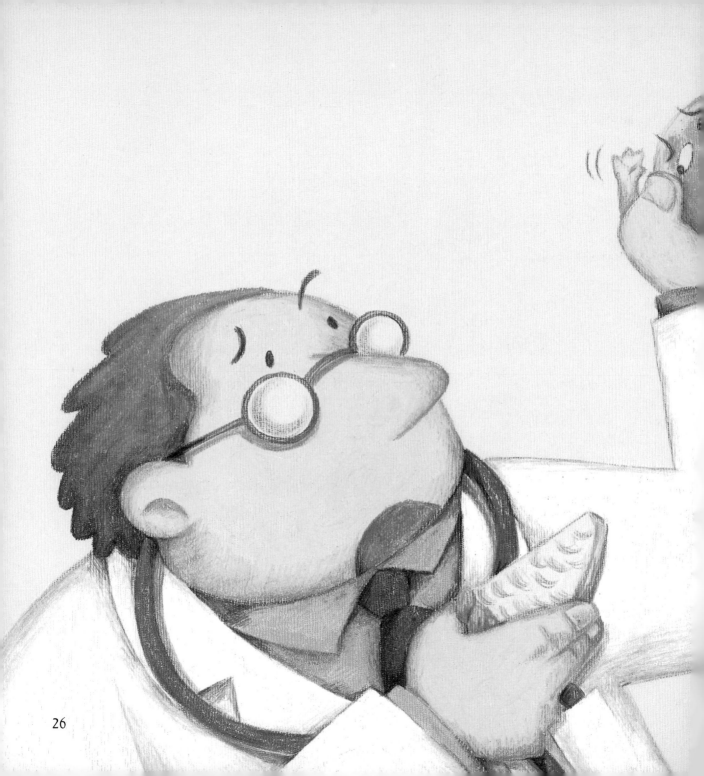

"Someone left food on my bed," he said.
The doctor was going to throw the food away
when Jim spoke to him.
"Don't throw me away! I was hoping you could help me.
I'm dying," said Jim.

「有人把食物留在我的床上。」他說。
醫生正想把它們丟掉時，吉姆開口說話了：
「別丟別丟！我快死了，希望你能救救我！」

"What did you say?" asked the doctor.

"I'm dying. Someone stole my jelly. A jelly doughnut cannot live without its jelly. Can you fix me so that someone will want to buy me? I used to be a handsome jelly doughnut once," said Jim.

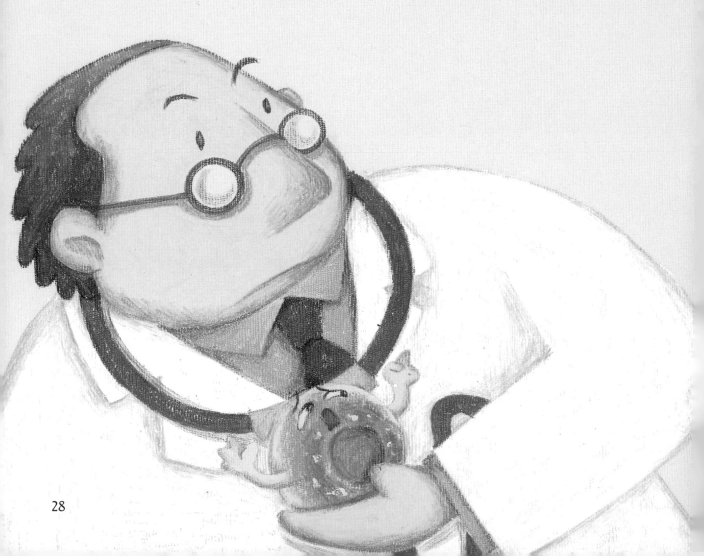

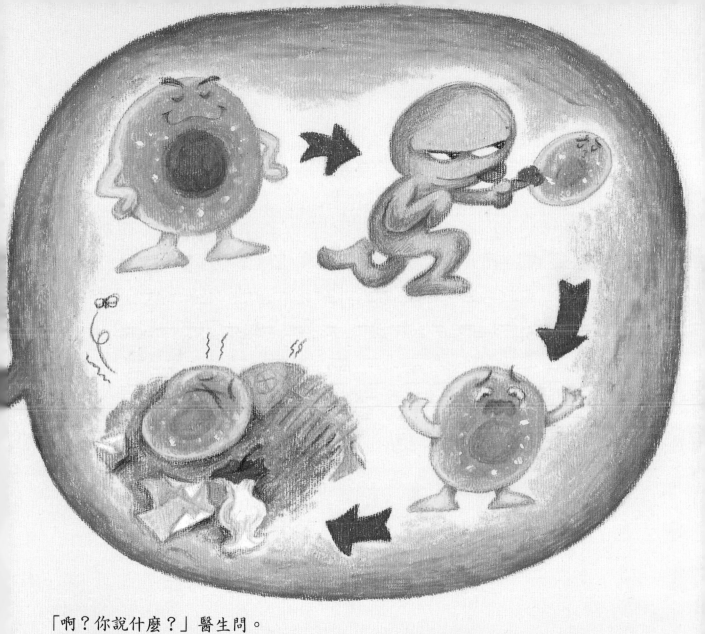

「啊？你說什麼？」醫生問。

「我快要死了，因為有人偷走了我的果醬。一個果醬甜甜圈沒有了果醬，
是活不下去的！你能把我治好嗎？這樣才會有人想把我買走。
我以前可是個很帥的果醬甜甜圈呢！」吉姆說。

"I cannot fix you. Only a baker can fix you.

He will give you some jelly," said the doctor.

"You mean, I am not going to die?" said Jim.

"Of course not, all you need is more jelly," said the doctor.

「我沒有辦法治好你,只有麵包師傅才能把你治好,

他會重新給你填一些果醬。」醫生說。

「你是說,我不會死囉?」吉姆說。

「當然不會囉!你只是需要再填一些果醬而已。」醫生回答。

The doctor took Jim back to the bakery.
He asked the baker to fix Jim.
The baker gave Jim some jelly so that
he became a perfect jelly doughnut again.

醫生把吉姆帶回麵包店，請麵包師傅把吉姆治好。
麵包師傅給吉姆填上一些果醬，
於是他又變成一個完美的果醬甜甜圈了！

Jim waited happily for someone to buy him.

At last some little boys came into the bakery.

Jim was excited. Little boys love jelly doughnuts.

Jim yelled, "Over here! Take me!"

"No, thank you. We don't eat junk food!" the boys said.

吉姆快樂地等著有人來把他買走。

最後，終於有一群小男孩走進麵包店裡。

吉姆好興奮呀！小男孩最喜歡果醬甜甜圈了！

吉姆喊著：「這裡這裡！快來買我呀！」

「不了，謝謝你，我們不吃沒營養的垃圾食物。」這群小男生說。

吉姆與蘋果派的大冒險

嗚嗚嗚……蘋果派！我的果醬又不見了！一定又是麵包師傅的兒子做的！

唉？他是麵包師傅的兒子去投外婆家，已經出門好幾天了，所以他應該不是兇手。

那…那到底是誰呢？我…我…我這次真得是死定了！麵包師傅又不在，拜託你幫我找兇手是誰！沒問題，交給我吧！我在這家麵包店裡待了這麼多年，也見過不少世面，這種小事應該難不倒我的！

蘋果派，我真是太感謝你了！謝謝你的路見不平、拔刀相助！

快別這麼說了！就讓我們看看到底是誰做的吧！

＊小朋友，玩這個遊戲時，可以準備一張紙，蓋住底下的路線圖，只露出起點。選定一個起點以後，就可以開始往下走了。在往下走的時候，隨著你走到的地方把蓋著的紙慢慢往下拉，這樣，你在走到叉路的時候，因為看不到下面的路，就要碰碰運氣，猜一猜哪條路才是正確的，玩起來會更刺激喔！

我們不吃垃圾食物啦！

你走錯了啦！

辛苦了，再走一次！

你來找找找看！

哈哈！好餓喔！

37

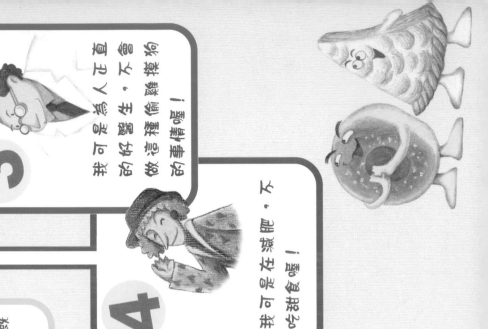

3 我可是正直的好醫生，不會做這種偷雞摸狗的事情喔！

4 我可是在減肥，不吃甜食喔！

2 才不是我們呢！我們這兒可是食物飲品，出入很遠喔！

5 嘿嘿！不好意思，被你抓到了！因為我會在大象慕你的果醬啦！哈哈！

1 別開玩笑了！我身上已經有令人心動的巧克力了，誰還要你的果醬！哈哈！

生字表

國家圖書館出版品預行編目資料

The Jelly Doughnut That Lost Its Jelly:失去果醬的
果醬甜甜圈 / Coleen Reddy著；倪靖繪；薛慧儀
譯.－－初版一刷.－－臺北市；三民，2003
        面；　公分－－(愛閱雙語叢書.二十六個妙朋
友系列) 中英對照
        ISBN 957-14-3769-7　　(精裝)

    1.英國語言－讀本

523.38   92008812

© The Jelly Doughnut That Lost Its Jelly
——失去果醬的果醬甜甜圈

著作人　Coleen Reddy
繪　圖　倪　靖
譯　者　薛慧儀
發行人　劉振強
著作財
產權人　三民書局股份有限公司
        臺北市復興北路386號
發行所　三民書局股份有限公司
        地址／臺北市復興北路386號
        電話／(02)25006600
        郵撥／0009998-5
印刷所　三民書局股份有限公司
門市部　復北店／臺北市復興北路386號
        重南店／臺北市重慶南路一段61號
初版一刷　2003年7月
    編　號　S 85643-1
    定　價　新臺幣壹佰捌拾元整
行政院新聞局登記證局版臺業字第○二○○號

ISBN　957-14-3769-7　　(精裝)